IT'S JUST NEWS

BECOME WANTED ENTERTAINMENT
PRESENTS

WORK ONE

A Story Created and Written by
DAVID GEARY

Cover Art Contributed by
DAVID GEARY

All rights reserved. No part of this book may be reproduced in any manner without written permission except in the case of brief quotations included in critical articles and reviews. For information, please contact the author.

Copyright © 2024 by
BECOME WANTED ENTERTAINMENT

Printed and Bound in the United States of America

All characters appearing in this work are fictitious.
Any resemblance to real persons, living or dead, is purely coincidental.

ISBN: 979-8-218-38439-5

All artwork including photography, cover art, and the Skyland's Finest logo Copyright © 2024 by
BECOME WANTED ENTERTAINMENT

BECOME WANTED ENTERTAINMENT
First Printing
www.becomewanted.com

CRAFTING A CHRONICLE

SKYLAND'S FINEST: WORK ONE

The thrill of crafting a compelling story for *Become Wanted Entertainment* lies in the limitless possibilities of Freeland City—a profound element that deeply intrigues me.

At the eye of our latest caper is Susan, a journalist whose path is set against the backdrop of Skyland's daring news and Freeland's sinister underbelly. This contrast is not just a setting—it's a character in its own right, enriching the narrative with complexity.

As the author, I've woven a tale that not only invites loyal fans back into the fold but also opens the door for new readers to explore the intricate web of relationships that have been the cornerstone of my storytelling.

So, I invite you to turn the page and dive into Susan's bold journey, where the stakes are higher and the bonds of friendship and courage are tested like never before.

David

A NEW DAWN

SKYLAND'S FINEST: WORK ONE

The low, ticking whirr of a tape recorder filled the room with an intangible monologue that had been playing on a loop throughout the night. A distinct voice, captured in the final moments of an interview, seeped into our young heroine's dreams, blending with the abstract landscapes of her slumber.

Her bedroom, a peaceful hideaway of warmth and reassurance, felt alive with the echoes of yesterday's work. Meanwhile, the tape recorder, an essential tool of her calling, sat dutifully on the nightstand, still turning as it replayed the Councilman's promises for Freeland City. The sound accessory was an unintentional soundtrack to her awakening and a reminder of a story she was piecing together, thread by journalistic thread.

A jotter, tucked beneath the soft glow beside the voice recorder, lay open, filled with pages that conveyed the marks of a journalist's restless pursuit of truth. Its corners were curled from periodic referencing while its

A NEW DAWN

pages were peeled back, revealing the layers of her strategic fact-finding approach. Each page was densely populated with a mixture of shorthand and straightforward script that only she could decipher. Similarly, the ink varied in intensity as if she was questioning a corrupt politician at a crossroads, a madman willing to share his secrets, or even a hero of the city reborn.

Across from the footboard of her bed, an antique wooden dresser stood proudly against one wall, adorned with personal snapshots arranged alongside a nifty box camera—a true pioneer of its kind. Her bedroom walls were modest and trimmed with care, pinned with the soft echoes of a career not yet professional but a stepping stone toward her goal. A meticulously crafted vision board portrayed a collage of objects that featured self-published articles on local events, profiles of the city's most notable heroes, and editorials on Freeland's issues that showcased her tenacity and

SKYLAND'S FINEST: WORK ONE

talent with the written word. These were the proving ground of her grit in the trenches of local news and community affairs, and while the walls lacked the prestige of a seasoned reporter, they were rich with the narrative of a woman's ambition to break into the competitive world of broadcast journalism.

Still clinging to the fading remnants of her *dreamy pie in the sky*, her eyes winked open in search of her reading glasses, which had tumbled off during the night's deep dive into her research. Therefore, with a tolerant stretch of her arm, she reached out to silence the Councilman mid-sentence, ending a story on the cusp of its grand finale.

Stripping down to her bare feet, she allowed the ways of the morning to envelop her. The bathroom, not spacious but a haven of simplicity, quickly filled with a searing yet soothing mist, erasing the lingering fog of sleep that had a hold on her. Though some favored evening showers, she found solace in

A NEW DAWN

her morning practice, which she believed was the best way to start any day. As she stood beneath the shower head mounted above her bottomless garden tub, water crashed over her neck and shoulders like shimmering raw diamonds, carrying with them the rejuvenating promise of a new dawn.

As the water stilled and the steam settled, the youthful newsy stood before the mirror, waiting for her reflection to appear through the dissipating vapors. There, she studied herself—a young woman defined by the stories she chased. Her hair varied in thickness and length, encasing her face with a touch of wild elegance just as her curious spirit mirrored in her steady gaze framed by fine dark lashes. Perhaps one of her most favorable features was her lips, poised for speech and eager for the next question. But lastly, perched on her small upturned nose were her reading glasses, a subtle indication of her nearsightedness that sweetened her smile.

SKYLAND'S FINEST: WORK ONE

Revealing a brief set of garments hanging in her closet, she weighed her options, brushing over various soft fabrics and fussy patterns until she decided on a look that exuded morale and charm, ideally suited for an opportunity that awaited her.

Inching toward the door, she gathered what appeared to be a beginner's portfolio when an incoming static sound of a buzzing radio propped up on her kitchen counter came to life.

"Good morning, Freeland! I'm Nancy Mae, your trusted newswoman, and today, I have a special announcement. After thirty-seven years here at Skyland News, I am retiring from my post.

As I gaze into the camera capturing this message, my silver hair reflects the wisdom and experience I've gained as a journalist in the field, and the countless hours I've spent surrendering my works with integrity and utmost honesty.

A NEW DAWN

Some things may never change about me, like this stunning navy blazer I am wearing, and marvelous string of pearls draped over me, which have become my trademark look over the decades.

It has been a privilege to serve as your source of information, and I am truly thankful for your trust and support. Furthermore, I would like to acknowledge this incredible news team for an outstanding run, and I have no doubt that Skyland will continue to uphold the highest standards of journalism.

As I say farewell, I invite the next generation of journalists to embrace the calling of becoming Skyland's Finest. The future of journalism is in your hands, and I have faith that you will carry on the legacy of delivering accurate, unbiased, and heartfelt news to the people of this city.

It has indeed been an honor. This is Nancy Mae, signing off. Goodbye and good luck, Freeland!"

FREELAND CITY

FREELAND CITY

Freeland, was a place where dreams came alive. It was a city rich in culture, sophistication, variety, and opportunity, embodying the very spirit and optimism of the swinging sixties. Freeland itself was a vast metropolis overflowing with a myriad spectrum of businesses, industries, and artistic institutions, for it was a hub of risk, innovation, and entertainment, reflecting the dynamic era in which it thrived.

Freeland's original greasy spoon, Yesturday's Jukebox Diner, was frequented by young and old alike, offering traditional meals under sweet melodies and the spirit of great service. Yesturday's was the backbone of the city's social scene, where its citizens gathered to share good fare and great conversation.

Past Perfect Curios was the choice for rare finds in Freeland City, with a name that evoked a sense of discovery. Known for its curated collection, each piece in the store had its own story, transforming every visit into a

SKYLAND'S FINEST: WORK ONE

journey back in time for collectors. Moreover, the store offered restoration services for antique items, ensuring that such objects were preserved for future generations and anyone fascinated by Freeland's vast history.

And finally, Gigi's Glamour Grove was the perfect haven of retro glamour and modern style, blending timeless beauty standards of the past with today's cutting-edge techniques. From classic cuts to current trends, Gigi's went beyond hair services by hosting monthly events and style workshops, fostering a community of creatives and beauty enthusiasts in Freeland.

What's more was Blue Dale's Bank at the center of the city's financial ward. As the premier capital institution, Blue Dale's played a pivotal role in managing the wealth of Freeland's thriving companies and affluent residents.

Alongside the automotive, oil, and telecommunication industries, Freeland's growth

FREELAND CITY

was greatly influenced by its printing, publishing, and manufacturing services. These initiatives played a significant role in driving the metropolis's economic prowess by providing employment opportunities while aiding in distributing information by producing academic periodicals, technical manuals, comic books, and the newspaper.

Together, these exceptional associations represented Freeland City, weaving a portrayal of prosperity felt in every corner, ensuring that the city remained not just a city of economic success but a beacon of hope and a testament to the power of unity and hard work.

A JOURNEY TO SKYLAND

A JOURNEY TO SKYLAND

Freeland's Samson Railway Station, the city's symbol of vibrant spirit, was an architectural marvel blending elements of the past and the sleek sophistication of the present in its design. The grand beginning showcased tall, arched stonework that whispered tales of the city's history. The interior shimmered with polished floors, contemporary fixtures, and a vast, breezy atmosphere, perfect for an open-air experience. Identified as an essential transportation hub, the station buzzed with activity at all hours, with Freeland's citizens relying on its wide network of commuter trains and subway lines to traverse the city.

Within the station, travelers found solace in the quaint amenities that lined the platform: small newsstands stocked with the latest papers and magazines, coffee shops that filled the air with the rich aroma of freshly brewed beverages, and a waiting area furnished with comfortable benches that invited passengers to rest their weary legs. It was in

SKYLAND'S FINEST: WORK ONE

one of these charming kiosks that our heroine would often procure her morning coffee, relishing the delicious scent as it mingled with the symphony of sounds emanating from the bustling station.

The magnificence of Samson Railway never ceased to inspire her, from the soaring open ceilings to the complex ironwork and the grand departures board. Thus, she made her way through the group of early goers, aiming to beat the growing coach line just in time for her train's arrival, and as the glorious steam locomotive drew near, a booming whistle resonated through the terminal, alerting the station's commuters of its approaching presence.

When the black locomotive sought the platform, a familiar face adorned with a silvery beard and crinkled laugh lines beamed with an amiable smile as he surveyed the crowd in search of someone extraordinary.

"Susan!"

A JOURNEY TO SKYLAND

Leaning out the operator's window, the train conductor greeted her with an expression that twinkled with the wisdom of countless journeys.

"Good morning, Ben!" Her voice was warm with gratitude, and her smile mirrored his own.

"Well aren't you dressed for an adventure?"

"I'm looking forward to a new chapter in my life," she spoke. "How do I look?"

Moved by her kind spirit, Ben leaned in to share his thoughtful words, laced with hope and anticipation for the exciting course ahead.

"You look perfect, Susan. Now, climb aboard…it's your time."

The steam coach was a benchmark of the railway staff's dedication and commitment to their craft. Its impeccable maintenance and distinguished reputation ensured its passengers a smooth, swift, and comfortable ride.

SKYLAND'S FINEST: WORK ONE

Exploring the expanded passenger compartment, Susan finally settled in at a window seat for the long trip, and as the train sped onward, the steady hum of mulitple conversations provided a soothing backdrop while the cityscape outside her window transformed before her very eyes.

The sun had finally ascended, uncovering a remarkable ivory tower for all to see. Its rectangular glass panels with contrasting jet frames were arranged symmetrically throughout the structure to contribute to the building's sense of order and importance in the eyes of its onlookers.

Hence at the pinnacle of the marvelous design, Skyland News was proudly displayed, welcoming its anchormen and anchorwomen, columnists, and ink slingers alike to participate in the all-encompassing local news affairs and where Susan hoped to find her place among the finest in the city.

ENTERING SKYLAND NEWS

SKYLAND'S FINEST: WORK ONE

Susan's spirit raced as she stepped into the rapid epicenter of Skyland News. The open-concept headquarters was a hive of activity, with journalists, editors, and researchers furiously working on their latest stories. The bluster of ringing telephones, tapping typewriter keys, and pressing voices excited her as she marveled at the diverse group of professionals that made up Skyland's news crew.

Seasoned journalists worked alongside eager newcomers like herself, each contributing their unique skills and perspectives. Despite their differences, they were united by their tenacious dedication to informing the public.

As Susan explored the crawling workspace, she became growingly overwhelmed, and amidst the chaos in the fast-paced environment, a friendly associate, recognizing a kindred spirit, decided to reach out and offer support.

ENTERING SKYLAND NEWS

"Hey there!" Just in time, a bright-eyed copy editor arrived with a warm welcome, for she, too, was just beginning her journey in the world of journalism, as seen on her badge.

"Oh, hey!" Susan reacted. The thoughtful beginner quickly stood out from the others in the department. Her full and curly chestnut hair was absolutely adorable, and when she smiled, a modest brilliance emitted from her, enriching her chipper personality. Heedless of her cheery spirit, she also had an undeniable fascination for uncovering hidden stories, just as Susan did.

"The name's Jane, I'm your copygirl, and I'd be happy to help you around this place." Her personality was a mix of resolve and kindness that allowed her to wander the high-pressure environment of the newsroom with unwavering enthusiasm, and even though she was still learning the ropes herself, Jane's belief in the power of journalism made her a valuable addition to the team.

SKYLAND'S FINEST: WORK ONE

Similarly, Susan was just as passionate. Her eyes sparkled with readiness and wonder, evident in how she approached her work. She was eager to make her mark in reportage and broadcasting. Yet, it was apparent that Susan struggled with inner conflict and perhaps the fear of failure.

"Sure, and by the way…I'm Susan."

Working one's way through the departments that comprised Skyland Central, Susan witnessed the prying team, which dug deep into complex stories; the political unit, which analyzed and reported the latest government happenings; the sports division, which covered regular spectacles; the entertainment and lifestyle section, which lightened the daily news with engaging features; and finally, the print bloc, a limited group responsible for arranging Skyland's ever-evolving content across the news landscape.

Jane also introduced Susan to Skyland's unrelenting dedication to accuracy, integrity, and timeliness; it was the workplace standard. The fast-paced environment demanded that every team member be agile, adaptable, and prepared to follow a breaking story.

The newsroom's constant pressure and breakneck speed slowly took its toll on Susan. She felt her nerves fraying, her stomach twisting, and her mind racing to keep up. Yet, Susan knew her place was here, knowing she could thrive with hard work, determination, and support just as they do.

Along their path through the newsroom, Jane glanced cautiously from left to right before speaking privately.

"Susan, there's something important I need to tell you. It's about Vanessa Rooney." Susan's eyes instantly widened with curiosity, so she listened intently.

"Oh? What's up with her?"

"Well, she's been around for a long time and has quite a reputation. She's ambitious as she is cunning, and she'll do whatever it takes

SKYLAND'S FINEST: WORK ONE

to get ahead…you need to be careful around her." Susan's brows furrowed with concern. However, she strived to remain focused, for it was her first day.

"Why are you telling me this?"

"Because I've seen her ruin the careers of promising interns and junior reporters who got in her way, and I don't want the same thing to happen to you. You're talented, and I believe you have a bright future here at Skyland News." Susan nodded. Her expression was a mix of gratitude and apprehension. Yet, fear gradually began to wash over her like a looming cloud preparing to ruin a sunny day at the pool.

"Thank you for the heads-up; I'll be sure to stay out of her way. But how will I know when she's onto me?"

"You'll notice her icy demeanor, blonde hair, and calculating stare from a mile away. Trust your instincts, don't share too much about your work with her, and remember, I'm

ENTERING SKYLAND NEWS

here to help you sort through all this." Nearly petrified, Susan took a deep breath, bracing herself for a nasty encounter to come.

"Thank you, Jane. I'll do my best to stay focused on my work and not let her get to me."

"That's the spirit, Susan! I know you'll go far in this industry."

Arriving at an unspecified foyer, Jane looked over Susan and gently nudged her with genuine concern.

"Listen. Our Chief Editor can be a tough nut to crack, but just be yourself and show him your passion for journalism, just like I saw in you; you're perfect." With that, Jane left her in the dimly lit lobby to pursue the lonely path ahead.

With a watchful eye, Susan stepped forward, and within a second, she was struck by an intrusive smell that saturated the air. The walls enclosing her, once a vibrant white, had now yellowed due to years of exposure.

SKYLAND'S FINEST: WORK ONE

Not only that, the dying bulbs supporting the open space exposed a mob of shadows that seemed to follow her every move.

Having reached the end of a rather challenging journey, Susan took a deep breath, approached the chipped door and loose knob, and knocked gently. Three times, to be exact. Meanwhile, her heart pounded rapidly when a gruff voice came from within.

"Come in!"

Susan entered an office that seemed frozen in time as the wallpaper, curling at its edges, gave way to the decades it had clung to the walls. Dominating the room was an imposing oak work desk and a sagging bookshelf packed with news-related editorials fraying at their spines. Her surroundings were fatty with past narratives, both told and untold, but on the worn worktop displayed before Susan was a traditional walnut nameplate that proclaimed the occupant's identity with aged dignity: Dennis Aaron Woodard–Senior Editor.

ENTERING SKYLAND NEWS

"That's far enough." Presumably tall, Dennis was a mildly overweight man with a bit of a slouch. His skin was slightly weathered, and his hair was a disarray of unkempt salt-and-pepper strands, crowning a face that seemed to be a repository of unpublished writings. Not to mention that Dennis's duds were far from polished; they were an afterthought—a wrinkled work shirt with its sleeves pushed back and a tie that hung loosely, suggesting an informal command over his agency. "Hmm," he grunted. The chain smoker that he was, an amber glass ashtray overflowing with days-old cigarette butts, contributed to the rank smell in his ward.

Susan's stomach began to churn as she fought the urge to cough due to the lack of clean oxygen, and as her eyes begged to water, she couldn't let it slip away. Therefore, she focused on why she was there.

"Susan Winters," she spoke despite the irritation in her throat.

SKYLAND'S FINEST: WORK ONE

"I know who you are. Portfolio, please?" Taking her billfold, he quietly leafed through its contents until one writing snatched his attention. "This piece on the Councilman would fit nicely as a new column in tomorrow's edition." His voice was steady. Moreover, he was spot on.

"I agree," she said. The prospect of her work actually being published began to grow, as so did the interview.

"Well, Susan, my role here extends far beyond what you see. I curate content ideas, plan and assign stories, edit content, and ensure everything is on track with our production schedules. I oversee our whole editorial staff, freelancers included."

She was tempted. It was here, in this office drowning in publications and nicotine, that Susan's dream was calling out to her—loud, clear, and impossible to ignore.

"I understand, sir. My passion for journalism would make me an excellent fit for

ENTERING SKYLAND NEWS

your team." She was ready, and Dennis held the ticket to her air castle.

"Then tell me, Susan. How well do you handle pressure? Our deadlines can be quite demanding."

"I thrive under pressure," she replied. "I believe it brings out the best in my work." After a moment of stillness, Dennis gradually stood up and motioned towards the door.

"You just might be what I'm looking for, Susan," he disclosed. He was a man of many sayings and even more riddles. "Come with me…we're going to take a ride above the city." Intrigued, Susan allowed him to find the door and eagerly followed while he led the way.

Atop Skyland, Susan was stunned to see a unique aircraft with a pronounceable series of letters spelling *SKY-BIRD* illustrated on its airframe.

"Oh gosh, Dennis…we're going up in that?" she asked.

SKYLAND'S FINEST: WORK ONE

Her voice shook in dread, for the impossible was about to become possible.

"This is the best way to see what Freeland is truly about. Trust me."

Confused and curious, Susan couldn't help but question the situation, and as for Dennis, it was evident that he took great pride in it.

The newly built heliport was a circular platform made of steel, furnished with handrails and sizable steps leading to the well-crafted helicopter. It was the first of its kind.

Hence, live airborne broadcasting allowed his team to respond to breaking stories quickly and to inaccessible locations by ground transportation.

Susan took a deep breath before entering the cockpit, and once seated, she discovered a complex arrangement of buttons and switches on the panel in front of her.

"You're a pilot, Mr. Woodard?"

ENTERING SKYLAND NEWS

"That I am, Miss Winters." Then, with a practiced hand, Dennis initiated the Sky-Bird's blades, developing a rhythmic hum, leading to Susan's stomach dropping as the sensation of weightlessness overwhelmed her while the ground fell away. "Do you know what they say about flying?" he asked. Meanwhile, Susan's knuckles turned white from squeezing the armrests so tightly as if the sheer force of her grip could anchor her to solid ground.

"Entertain me, sir," she muttered through clenched teeth.

"It's just like riding a bike, except you're 1,000 feet in the air!"

MAYDAY

MAYDAY

Her screams pierced the air as the Sky-Bird soared over the city while her heart raced faster than the aircraft itself—meanwhile, a mischievous grin formed on Dennis's face.

"Oh, Susan, relax! I invested a great deal of money for you to have this experience! So, toughen up will ya?"

"Copy that," Susan fussed.

As they soared over the district, Dennis suddenly became Freeland's Sky-Guide, pointing out landmarks and sharing stories about its history.

"Look over there!" Dennis knew how to show rather than tell as she recognized the crowded street below.

"That's my street!" Susan exclaimed. The Chief Editor's persistence and contagious enthusiasm finally paid off, transforming Susan's fear into joy. "The view from above is stunning; it's as though Freeland's skyline stretches on forever."

"That's where I got my first big scoop as

SKYLAND'S FINEST: WORK ONE

a reporter, and in that building to your right is where we exposed the biggest political scandal in Freeland's history."

The thrill of being up in the sky was unlike anything she'd ever experienced before, and there, she learned to laugh along with Dennis while he told more jokes.

"You know, Susan," he began, "I can see that same hunger for stories in you that I had when I first started out, and I would love to see that burning desire under my watch...welcome to the team."

Susan's spirit swelled with triumph. She couldn't believe Skyland's Chief Editor had offered her the opportunity she longed for.

"Thank you, Dennis—I won't let you down!"

"I know you won't, Susan." He, too, was proud, for he could sense the story chaser in her, the desire for the hunt he relinquished long ago.

While the bold Sky-Bird soared on, they

MAYDAY

began to share accounts of amusement, with one, Susan, knowing this was just the beginning of her adventures with Dennis and the team at Freeland City's most prestigious newspaper.

As Susan disembarked from the Sky-Bird, her happiness from the incredible adventure with Dennis was nearly tangible. But then, while leaving his office, her euphoria was short-lived as she met the stormy newswoman whose reputation preceded her.

"I see he has taken a liking to you." As Jane noted, her blonde hair, piercing blue eyes, and ideology of sophistication projected an intimidating aura that kept many colleagues at bay. Thus, with a forced smile, she offered a seemingly friendly greeting.

"Vanessa, delighted to finally meet you."

"Don't."

"Okay."

Her personality was a complex mix of ambition, cunningness, and cruelty. Hence,

SKYLAND'S FINEST: WORK ONE

she held no punches in addressing Susan.

"I hope you enjoyed your little joyride; *mayday-mayday* boom." Taken aback by Vanessa's cold demeanor, Susan steeled herself while selecting her following words.

"It was great! I've never seen the city from up there, let alone from an actual helicopter. Heck, you can't catch views like that from the train," she poked.

Far from listening, Vanessa's relentless crusade for success often led her to employ questionable tactics, earning her a reputation as a problematic team player and, perhaps, an even more difficult co-partner.

"There's more to this job than scenic helicopter rides," she mentioned. "You'll need to prove you have what it takes to survive in this business."

"I get that. I simply want to make a difference here." Susan's guard slowly began to crumble as she sensed Vanessa's underlying hostility seeping out.

MAYDAY

"We'll see," she scoffed, "Just remember, I've been here for over thirteen years, and I won't let some rookie take this station's top spot." Since Nancy Mae announced her retirement, many had been eyeing the coveted position, and Vanessa was determined to claim it at any cost.

Susan could sense the tension surge as she realized that Vanessa now viewed her as a threat. Therefore, she was careful to maintain her composure.

"I'm not here to step on anyone's toes, Vanessa. I just want to do my job and tell important stories."

"Perfect," she sneered, and as she leaned in closer, her voice became a hissing whisper, only for the ears of Susan Winters. "This newsroom isn't big enough for both of us, so stay out of my way."

"Sure."

Vanessa's words carried a venomous bite while her sharp stare snared Susan, unwilling

SKYLAND'S FINEST: WORK ONE

to release her until her arm-twisting threat was achieved.

"See you around."

With that, she marched away, exuding a ferocious elegance like a sharp-set lioness disappearing into the maze of desks.

As for Susan, her sense of newfound glory had just crashed. The gravity of Vanessa Rooney's warning loomed over her like a dense mass settling upon the entire building. She couldn't ignore the reality that Skyland's lead news anchor was capable of anything, even if it meant snuffing out the flame of her purpose.

SETTLING IN

SKYLAND'S FINEST: WORK ONE

Excitement bubbled in Susan's heart as she docked her heels at the busy entry of Skyland News. The morning air was crisp, filled with the endearing scent of autumn, declaring the start of a new season and a fresh beginning for her journalism career. Thus, with a worthy note bag slung over her shoulder, she embraced the thrill of her first official day on the job.

Exploring the foyer, she took in the details of a fabulous waiting area that blended elements of modernity with the magnetism of a bygone era, and at the center of it all, a receptionist greeted her with an incredible compliment that had swept the office.

"Dennis couldn't have made a finer decision...welcome to Skyland, Ms. Winters."

Skyland's finest watchwoman, equipped with a zeal that never faltered, inspired the foyer with her spreadable character and gorgeous features, while her elegant demeanor granted her an ageless charm. Her brown hair,

SETTLING IN

falling in soft waves around her shoulders, allowed her vibrant green eyes to sparkle, plus her style, a brilliant combination of experience and chic that mirrored her personality, complemented with a touch of jewelry, not too flashy but just enough to add a hint of sophistication, magnified her position as she received each person who walked through the door.

"I see you're up to the task on your first day?"

"Yes, I am! I stopped by Yesturday's for breakfast, and let me tell you, their Eggs Benedict was—"

But before she could engage in further chatter, her eyes were suddenly drawn to a fascinating character who reeked of tobacco and pretentiousness.

"Out of my way, you simpletons!" He was a cranky someone whose voice shook nearly everyone in the lobby, including Susan. In comparison, the watchwoman was utterly

SKYLAND'S FINEST: WORK ONE

unimpressed as she stood unafraid of the fabricated man who called himself Freeland's Press Pioneer. "Can't this news station write better stories?"

Bedecked in a regal dress garment with a three-inch tall collar tailored to fit his wide neck, akin to the trunk of a robust tree, the shortage of separation of his throat and jawline emphasized the weight he harbored as if the burden of his endeavors had melded his neck and face into a single solid presence. Over and above, his massive head was stuffed in a low crown double felt poll hat while his solid shoulders hid seamlessly beneath a sturdy overcoat that swallowed his entire body. But, behind the man's scowling face, his narrow eyes, peering through the glass of his round nose-pinchers, seemed to hold an unsettling depth as if he could see through the facade of anyone caught in his path.

"I'm sorry, sir," she winced.

"Sorry?" Suddenly, with a curt nod, he

SETTLING IN

stopped to acknowledge her brave existence. "Don't be sorry," he muttered. "I trust you'll find a way to meet the lofty standards set by Inkwell," he stated. "Welcome to Skyland, and you have a fine day."

"Thank you, sir," she whispered as she watched the man who disturbed everyone in attendance exit the building.

Susan couldn't help but feel a sharp coldness. She learned that beneath his facade of success and influence lay a figure who spared no one from his petulance and made it clear that he had little regard for the feelings or opinions of those around him.

"Who was that?"

"Graves, dear. He is the founder of Inkwell Press & Company, Skyland's only alternative since his competitors have all fallen from the industry.

"You mean he is the person who prints the newspaper?"

"Yes, now run along…you wouldn't want

43

SKYLAND'S FINEST: WORK ONE

to be late to your desk on your first day."

"Right…and your name is?"

"Linda, darling." After surviving Graves, Susan couldn't help but smile. Despite the years Linda had spent behind her desk, as etched on her facility badge, her eagerness for the task remained undiminished, for she was the first to arrive and the last to leave, an authentic dedication to her role even more evident that she was more than Skyland's receptionist; she was its beating heart.

"Well, it was a pleasure meeting you, and I look forward to hearing your story, Linda." Stepping off in the direction of two swinging doors to the newsroom, Linda reminded Susan to punch in.

"Over there, honey!" In one corner stood the time clock, an old-fashioned punch card device that employees used to record their arrival and departure times, where she joined the line of associates, each offering a friendly gesture while she waited.

SETTLING IN

Reviewing the newsroom, Susan marveled at the interior blend of sleek lines and functional simplicity characteristic of the times. Overhead lights bathed the workspace, during which large windows offered stunning views of the bustling city beyond. The workstations were arranged in an open concept, fostering collaboration between the various departments just as the walls provided iconic pieces from Skyland's storied past, proof of the newspaper's commitment to journalistic excellence.

Susan was amazed. As she passed by each article, she felt inspired by a legacy—now a part of, and the potential for her work to someday grace the same walls, and with each step she took, her warmth for the distinguished firm grew.

Passing the production department, Jane welcomed her, who had taken an interest in her new working environment experience thus far.

SKYLAND'S FINEST: WORK ONE

"I knew Dennis was going to choose you the moment we met."

"Thank you. This all seems unbelievable, and yet, here I am...still getting used to it all." Jane nodded, understanding the eagerness of a newcomer.

"You'll find your stride. Oh, by the way, I almost forgot to tell you—your new desk and chair arrived, and everyone's been talking about the fantastic take of Freeland's skyline from your spot. It should be a nice source of inspiration."

Susan's eyes lit up at the mention of the sky view. She had always found solace in the vastness of the stratosphere and its ever-changing hues. It supplied her with a sense of perspective when faced with challenging situations.

"I'm looking forward to settling in and making the most of my first day. Thanks again, Jane."

"You got it!"

SETTLING IN

Joining the designated space for lead newshounds, Susan discovered her desk, a sturdy oak piece with a slightly vintage look, near the largest window on the floor. It was simple yet significant, a perfect reflection of her. The view from her standing was indeed inspiring, offering the finest vantage point of Freeland's cityscape, but waiting silently behind her workstation was a fashionable chair known for its mélange presentation of stable features and nuanced blends of rich yarns, ready to support her through early mornings and long nights of diligent work to come.

Unloading her note bag, she carefully arranged her notebook, photo references, and favorite ink pens. Thus, her little corner in the world of journalism became the beginning stage of this journey, and as she sat down, she felt a warm sense of belonging.

Yet, from a calculated distance outside the limits of the newsroom, the icy anchor, draped in an aura of cold excellence, observed

SKYLAND'S FINEST: WORK ONE

Susan, who had seemingly charmed everyone in the facility, including the grump, Graves.

Analyzing her every move, a scornful smirk played on her lips as she recalled her first day when she had that same burning ambition that had fueled her rise in the competitive world of journalism behind the very desk that once belonged to her. Those were the days—but years of competition and cutthroat politics had hardened her, turning her initial passion into an unquenchable thirst for control.

THE PAPER'S PULSE

SKYLAND'S FINEST: WORK ONE

At the stroke of noon, a ballet of machinery played out beneath the high ceilings of the notorious Inkwell Press and Company. Within its walls, the giant metal plates, engraved with tales and happenings, spun gracefully on their cylinders, a symphony of industry that inked Skyland's publication onto sheets of paper. The scent of fresh ink hung thick in the air, a perfume for the artisans of information who worked tirelessly amidst the cacophony of gears and rollers.

Into this hive of activity strode Graves, commanding the roaring machines around him simply with his presence. Heralding his entry, a plume of tobacco smoke followed him, weaving through the building like a spectral serpent, a stark contrast to the mechanical precision that dominated the room.

"Good day, Mr. Sinclair." The voice of the main-line supervisor cut through the din like a well-worn blade through thick fabric, as though it held a certain depth with a firmness

THE PAPER'S PULSE

that demanded acknowledgment and consideration from those within earshot.

"Manny." His reaction was rather dismissive, for his attention had already drifted to the flurry of activity that defined his empire. The uproar of the workroom enveloped him, a racket that might overwhelm some, but for Graves, it was a symphony of productivity.

"Tomorrow's paper will be ready in precisely four minutes, sir." He was a withering man with a lifetime of labor etched on his face, neck, and hands. Covered in rugged garments like the devoted workmen behind him, Manny was yet admired for his understanding of the inner workings of the unstoppable forge and, perhaps, even Graves, who, too, valued the age-old man.

"Excellent."

As he moved with deliberate steps, his employees, stained with the day's work, stole glances at him, distracted by the trail of smoke that followed him like a phantom tide.

SKYLAND'S FINEST: WORK ONE

These hard-working citizens were the cogs in his grand machine, each playing their part to ensure the news would flow through the city's veins like lifeblood.

Standing at the heart of the press floor, he allowed himself a moment of pride. The steady thudding of the machines and his empire's heartbeat seemed in perfect sync with his own. His trade was more than a factory; it was the heart and marrow of the city's transmission of communication felt throughout Freeland.

As the first batch of newspapers made their way off the line, haze, rivering from his lips, seemed to infuse with the paper and ink while he gave Manny an almost unseeable nod to carry on. The article would publicize sayings of Michael Gibson's latest capers and introduce Susan Winters as the new voice to resonate within Skyland News, with Graves overseeing it all.

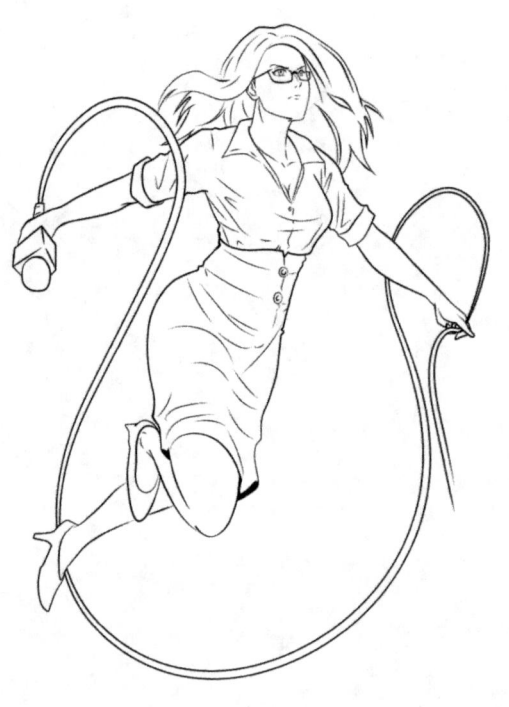

*SETTLING IN
(CONTINUED)*

SKYLAND'S FINEST: WORK ONE

Three hours later, Susan was deeply entrenched in the humdrum of seemingly inconsequential tales. Her assignments, comprising minor traffic snarl-ups, a lukewarm response to the local gardening club's annual flower affair, and a brief note on the new offerings at a renowned gelateria, may not have been thrilling, but they did form the bedrock of Skyland News' trustworthiness in covering the community's day-to-day affairs. Yet, as Susan delved deeper, a sense of discontent gnawed at her. She had envisioned her role at Skyland as a strengthened crusader, unearthing dramatic revelations and chasing pivotal leads. Instead, the reality of her role seemed far removed from her lofty ambitions.

In her introspective moment, Susan's attention was caught by a piece that rekindled her journalistic fervor. It was a chronicle tracing the relentless battle against organized crime waged by Freeland City's celebrated Detective, Michael Gibson. His audacious

SETTLING IN (CONTINUED)

escapades and unwavering pursuit of justice reignited Susan's commitment to impactful journalism.

"Sampling the local news flavor, I see?" Jane's sudden appearance nearly shook Susan, prying her away from the compelling narrative.

"Yeah…you could say that."

"Speaking of flavors, have you checked out Skyland's cafeteria yet? The food there is amazing!" Susan, while offering a tentative smile, seemed uncertain.

"I've heard institutional food can be hit or miss."

"Believe me, our cafeteria is a culinary oasis. The chefs are committed to using fresh produce, and they curate a diverse menu that caters to a spectrum of palates. Besides, it's a wonderful spot to unwind and engage in conversations with your fellow journalists." Susan, still skeptical, arched an eyebrow in response.

SKYLAND'S FINEST: WORK ONE

"I suppose a break from these articles is needed. What do you suggest?"

"Their meatloaf is a culinary masterpiece, and the sandwiches are consistently delightful. But, you absolutely must savor their apple pie…it's a local legend!" Susan's laughter, spurred by Jane's infectious enthusiasm, echoed through the department.

"Alright, you've convinced me! Let's head over there and see if the food lives up to your praises."

"Excellent! You're in for a treat. And while we're there, we can explore that piece on Mr. Gibson; I have a few intriguing anecdotes to share."

SKYLAND'S FINEST: WORK ONE

The Press Plate, lodged within the thriving gut of Skyland News, had been a haven for journalists, editors, and media personnel since its inception. The cafeteria's well-ordered ambiance mirrored the pulse of the new station itself, always alive and always buzzing.

Its story began in 1951 when it was conceived by the then editor-in-chief of Skyland News, Franklin Webb. A man of wit and wisdom, Webb wanted to create a space that would not only satiate the hunger of his dedicated staff but also serve as a melting pot for ideas and discussions, where stories were not just consumed but also created.

The cafeteria was designed to reflect a newsroom's eclectic nature with its long, rustic tablelands and mismatched chairs. The walls were embellished with framed front pages of meaningful documented events. The aroma of freshly grounded coffee beans, the clang of cutlery, and the hum of mur-

mured conversations created a symphony that fueled the heartbeat of Skyland News.

The kitchen, located at the nucleus of the cafeteria, was the belly of The Press Plate, and it was here that the magic truly happened. The kitchen staff, led by the indomitable Chef Kenneth Clifton, was best known for their ability to swirl up mouth-watering meals at lightning speed. However, their position at the hub of the Press Plate served more than just a practical purpose. It symbolized the fundamental belief that physical and intellectual nourishment was at the crux of journalism and a beacon for those who believed in the power of the press.

"You know, Michael Gibson is a real-life hero. He's put away some of the most dangerous criminals in Freeland, like the notorious mobster, Frankie 'King Fish' Delano. I've heard that the police department is incredibly grateful for his help." While appreciating Jane's enthusiasm, Susan forks a moment,

SKYLAND'S FINEST: WORK ONE

takes a bite of her meatloaf, and nods, urging Jane to continue. "The Freeland City Police Department was knee-deep in unsolved cases until he came along. He's got this uncanny ability to solve even the most complex crimes. It's like he's always one step ahead of everyone else."

"That's world-class, no doubt about it. But we should also remember that the police department itself is full of dedicated officers working hard to keep the city safe, wouldn't you agree?"

"Oh, absolutely! But you have to admit, he adds a flair to crime-solving. It's almost like he's a character straight out of a Detective novel." Susan, amused by Jane's enthusiasm, finally indulges the copygirl's compulsive curiosity.

"Alright, I'll bite. What's your favorite story about Detective Gibson?" Suddenly, Jane's eyes twinkle with ado as she calls up her number one report about Freeland's hero.

TALES FROM THE CAFÉ

"Okay, I have to tell you about the time he stopped Danny from taking Blue Dales Bank. It's one of my absolute faves!" Susan, curious about the story, encourages Jane to continue.

"Go on."

"Danny Black and his crew were infamous criminals, known for their hate for the police and meticulous planning in burglary. At the beginning of this story, they had already robbed three banks, leaving no traces behind, and when they targeted Blue Dales Bank, they thought it would be just another job."

"I take it they were mistaken?"

"Oh, they had no idea what they were in for! When Michael had caught wind of their scheme, he spent weeks learning their methods until he discovered a pattern in their heists, and that is how he predicted when and where their next thievery would take place."

"Quite impressive, given that they had

always managed to evade the authorities."

"Indeed! Therefore, the great Detective, on the day of the robbery, alerted the Freeland City Police Department and had them secretly stationed around the institution at the moment Danny and his boys broke in."

"So, what happened next?" Susan asked.

"As the robbers began to loot the place, the police sprang into action, and apprehended those thugs, sending their leader on the run, and our hero himself to pursue after him. But to the crook's surprise, he ran into a tight fix and with no escape route due to the Detective's masterful design. Then, Danny did the unthinkable."

"What did he do?"

"Let me finish, Susan, gosh." Overjoyed to have an audience at this point, Jane took full advantage by asking a listening colleague to refill her glass of soda before continuing. "Thank you, kindly," she inferred. "So, where was—oh yeah! Running out of time, Danny did the unthinkable and broke his own two legs and managed to squeeze through a crack in the wall before Michael could catch him."

"You mean he was never captured?"

"Yup! Despite all of Michael's efforts, Danny Black remains at large to this day. He's become something of a legend in the criminal underworld, but it's also a warrant to the great Detective's craftwork that he was able to dismantle his wicked agenda."

By the end of Jane's story, Susan's jaw dropped in awe. The story of Michael stopping Danny, albeit not capturing him, only reinforced her admiration for his extraordinary crime-solving abilities, thus, adding another layer of intrigue to the city of Freeland.

The Press Plate was buzzing with laughter and cheer due to Jane's rare ability to hold an audience. However, Susan, still swirling with craves of Freeland's strong-willed Detective in action, managed to slip away. She

SKYLAND'S FINEST: WORK ONE

couldn't help but wonder what it would be like to be amid such dangerous investigations.

As Susan reached her desk, she noticed an anomaly amidst her neat arrangement that hadn't been there before she left. She glanced around the newsroom with suspicion. But to her dismay, the department was empty.

Suddenly, a creeping sense of curiosity rushed over her as she fixed her eyes upon a mysterious dark-blue dossier. The silence around her was gradually replaced by the uninviting pounding of her heart, for the dossier was unmarked, which sent a flutter of rarity through her entire body.

THE MYSTERIOUS DOSSIER

SKYLAND'S FINEST: WORK ONE

Its blue cover radiated mystery against the backdrop of her neatly arranged post supplies. Subtly taped to the front was a small handwritten message alluding to something far more intriguing than the mundane stories she had been working on.

Since lunch at The Press Plate, Jane's first-hand narrative of the great Detective still lingered in Susan's mind, echoing impressions of greatheartedness and noteworthy journalism, and consequently, Michael's relentless pursuit of justice and fearlessness in the face of danger stirred something within her as she mustered the same courage to explore the silent ledger,

Then, as bravery splashed with curiosity, Susan reached for the puzzle purse. She couldn't help but wonder if this was the opportunity she had been waiting for, a chance to make her mark at Skyland News and pursue the kind of journalism she had always dreamed of.

THE MYSTERIOUS DOSSIER

As she peeled the note from the dossier, she read the cryptic message:

"Tread carefully."

Her heart sprinted at the potential implications of this information. If Freeland's hero, Michael Gibson, could face danger and adversity in his fight for justice, then perhaps she could do the same.

In the time Susan traced the cold surface of the dossier with her fingertips, a surge of anticipation coursed through her. All that mattered was the mysterious contents in her hand, and as she carefully opened it—

"Oh my god," she spoke.

Inside was a jigsaw of police reports, witness statements, photographs, and hastily scribbled notes from confidential interviews, each piece a tantalizing clue about the elusive asset, adding to the complexity of a story that promised to be anything but ordinary.

SKYLAND'S FINEST: WORK ONE

Swept up in the thrill of the unknown, the words flickered before her eyes as she read, weaving a story of intrigue, danger, and the promise of truth yet to be unveiled.

The Phantom Wallet, a codename used in hushed whispers among the criminal underbelly of Freeland, acted as a wraith that seemed to function at the center of a web of illicit activities across the city.

Then, as the late hour dawned, the dying light crept in through the office windows, and the once lively newsroom became a shadow of its daytime self, with only a few dedicated souls like Susan still at their desks.

Her mind teemed with possibilities while her beating spirit matched its tempo. What secrets did the arcane archive hold? Who was daring enough to leave such a damning trail of evidence in plain sight? These questions required answers, and Susan knew one thing was for certain. Her life at Skyland was about to get a whole lot more interesting.

THE MYSTERIOUS DOSSIER

Clung to both adventure and possible jeopardy, Susan realized she was on the cusp of something monumental that could forever alter her career trajectory at Skyland News. Therefore, she finished scanning the contents of the covert carrier and carefully slipped it into her bag, safely hidden from prying eyes.

Lastly, amidst the newshounds tirelessly questing for the truth, Susan quietly left her desk, poised to delve into the labyrinthine riddle begging to be solved.

THE SET-UP

THE SET-UP

The city's public archive, a grand, historic building with marble columns and a towering clock, held the chronicles of Freeland's rich history. It was here that Susan hoped to uncover the truth behind the mysterious billfold.

The loftiness of the reading room, with its elevated awnings lined with ornate moldings and walls adorned with portraits of Freeland's most influential figures, filled her with awe and anticipation.

As she approached the reference desk, Susan witnessed a brass nameplate with engraved letters that spelled out: Mr. Harrington resting under the soft glow of the workstation's study lamp.

Gazing beyond the writing station, she was suddenly greeted by a small, passionate man with a crown of white hair and a keen monocle wedged between his soft cheek and lower right eyebrow, giving him an air of wisdom and refinement.

SKYLAND'S FINEST: WORK ONE

"First time at the archive, I presume?" he said, his voice faint yet unmistakable.

"Yes, sir," she expressed while her eyes wandered at the endless rows of information encircling them.

"I can see the zeal in your eyes, young lady," he spotted. "It's not even eight yet, and you're here…that's the spirit of a true researcher." Susan was immediately put at ease by his gracious welcome. The twinkle in his eyes and his eagerness to assist her created a comforting atmosphere. It was a stark contrast to the competitive environment she had already experienced back at Skyland News.

"Well, I'm Susan." He made it easy for her as she smiled in return to acquire his liking, "I'm looking for some materials related to an investigation I'm currently working on," she then shared. At the time, she held close the secretive item stowed in her note bag slung over her shoulder.

THE SET-UP

"Well, Susan," his eyes crimped at the corners as he grinned, "you've come to the right place. We have a wealth of information here, waiting to be discovered."

With a canvas configuration of the archive already in grasp, the kind man stepped away from his studies to direct Susan to the section suited for her exploration.

"Thank you again, Mr. Harrington."

"Sure."

She began pulling books, searching for clues to aid her in piecing together the lockbox disguised as the blue dossier. She took detailed notes and cross-referenced her findings, gradually building a clearer picture of the web of intrigue surrounding the scandal.

"C'mon, something must fall," she whispered. As the day wore on, Susan became more engrossed in her research, when eventually, the ledger mentioned a piece of evidence located in the very building in which she had stood for the past six hours. "Bingo."

SKYLAND'S FINEST: WORK ONE

Darting into each aisle, she located the text and opened it to find a foolish red flag with an attached note that simply sounded:

"Gotcha!"

"Not funny." Snatching the streamer and closing the book, Susan made her way to the exit, passing Mr. Harrington in bother.

"Be well, Susan Winters," he spoke.

The realization that this was an elaborate prank orchestrated by Vanessa hit Susan like a ton of bricks. Her imagined colleagues snickering in the newsroom, her wasted time and effort away from Skyland, and Vanessa's crowing smirk on set before the evening's broadcast ripped the excitement of potentially uncovering a powerful story, giving way to humiliation and self-doubt.

NEWS FLASH

"Graves," also known to some as Lucius Sinclair, is a man of intriguing contradictions whose physical appearance mirrors the burdens he carries, both literal and metaphorical. Despite his imperfections, Lucius possesses unwavering grit, earthborn resilience, and a mind as sharp as a dagger. A student of time and secrets, he is bound to leave an indelible mark on the city's twisted history while establishing his legacy for he is the founder of Vintage Inkwell Press & Company.

EXTRA

Hidden beneath Graves' cranky deception lies a well-guarded illness, a clandestine sickness that even the most tenacious physicians have failed to untangle.

DID YOU KNOW

A man of refined taste, Graves takes solace in his treasured collection of hand-carved wooden pipes, each weathered with time and etched with memories as a testament to the ongoing disorder that overshadows Freeland City.

NEWS FLASH
Among those who attended Nancy Mae's retirement transmitted from the greatest story network, Skyland News, Susan Winters, a daring journalist with a longing for fairness and an eye for danger, stepped up to seize the chance at becoming the city's next beloved reporter. Yet, little does she know that great journalism not only demands a commitment to the citizens of Freeland but requires sheer bravery, resourcefulness, and the wit to survive scenarios that many before her have not.

EXTRA
Unbeknownst to Susan Winters, her ambition to become Skyland's Finest will thrust her into a world far darker and more treacherous than she could ever imagine.

DID YOU KNOW
Beyond her tenacious pursuit of becoming Skyland's Finest, Susan seeks enlightenment in East Freeland every Summer, honing her skills in Judo to further instill discipline, resilience, and self-defense.

NEWS FLASH
Messengers are highly trained combatants who are only summoned when outsiders threaten to unravel the sinister riddles that the Inked Brotherhood aspires to defend. Hand-selected by a high-ranking member of the organization, Monroe has proven to be one of their most valuable assets, for he is committed to delivering cryptic messages and purging those who seek to jeopardize the secrecy of the Brotherhood.

EXTRA
Before assuming his role as a Messenger, Monroe's memories, personal history, and even his birth name were meticulously erased and replaced with the organization's intricate design and a lengthy list of targets.

DID YOU KNOW
Despite his dark and secretive nature, Monroe has a keen eye for fine art, for he is a profound collector, finding inspiration and solace in the beauty of the pieces he purchases.

*THE SET-UP
(CONTINUED)*

SKYLAND'S FINEST: WORK ONE

Standing before Skyland News, Susan held her head high, but inside, she was in ruins. In her hand was the red flag, pinched between two fingers, unable to shake off the false scandal that unfolded at the city's archive. Upon her return, she felt the suppressed laughter of Vanessa, who appeared wearing a rather expensive designer suit, lingering near her things.

"Oh, hey!" she put on, "You're back!" The nasty woman's words were an attack, not to be mistaken, "How was your little…experience?" Her voice was a poisoned honey trickling with condescension, "I'm sure Mr. Harrington loaned you his utmost attention in showing you around." Once a symbol of aspiration and potential, Skyland News had become an outright battleground.

The bated whispers of her colleagues felt like feathers brushing against her skin, each one a reminder of her public humiliation. However, Susan was then collected,

THE SET-UP (CONTINUED)

although she sensed a whirlwind of emotions clashing within her.

"I see you had some fun at my expense," Susan spoke. Yet, Vanessa's presence, meant to isolate and belittle her, had hit its mark. Her breath hung in the air like suffocating smoke, during which the prickling sensation of tears threatened to escape Susan's eyes as she swallowed hard to steady her anger.

"Oh, c'mon, Susan, it was just a silly initiation, after all…we're a team here, right?" The newsroom had never felt so unsafe. The clattering keys of typewriters, the constant ringing of incoming calls, the rustling of papers, every sound seemed magnified. Even Jane, whom she had connected with on her first day, would not meet her gaze. Therefore, the lack of support from someone she considered an ally was an even harsher blow. But then—

"VANESSA!" At the sound of his voice, the circus spun away in fear of—

SKYLAND'S FINEST: WORK ONE

"WHAT, DENNIS!" she shouted.

"My office, NOW!" And just like that, the chief editor's voice struck the department, summoning the bitter anchor to his cigarette box for a command, and as for Susan, she was permitted to take back her desk in the end.

Susan had envisioned her role at Skyland News differently. She pictured breaking incredible stories and becoming an integral part of the team. But instead, she became the punchline behind a cruel prank that had left her feeling vulnerable and alone.

INTRIGUE ON TAP

SKYLAND'S FINEST: WORK ONE

As the sun dipped below the horizon, Susan wandered toward JJ's Tavern, indicated above its wooden single entry. The air was relatively calm, perhaps hinting a storm to come, whereas the sweaty streets mirrored the last rays of sunlight across the city.

Nestled between a paint store and an empty alley, its warm flickering neon sign, mounted in the window, welcomed the weary with the promise of refuge from the testy world outside, and as our cheerless journalist found the entrance, a tattered newspaper fluttered past her to find its place around an aluminum trash bin near the door giving way to the end of a stormy workday.

Upon entering the tavern for the first time, Susan's emotions were a turbulent mix of betrayal and doubt. She hesitated momentarily, taking in the scene before her, then chose a stool at the end of the bar, hoping for a quiet corner to nurse her wounds.

"What can I get you?"

INTRIGUE ON TAP

Behind the counter stood the barkeeper. A stocky man in his mid-fifties with salt-and-pepper hair, he had a kind face that had seen its fair share of laughter and sorrow. His eyes creased at the ends, evidence of countless stories shared and secrets kept. The bar was dimly lit, casting shadows on the aged wooden floors and mismatched furniture. The walls were adorned with memorabilia from bygone eras, each a witness to the souls seeking solace here.

"A whiskey sour, please," Susan replied, a classic choice befitting the moment after her troublesome workday.

"Sure, and the name's JJ."

"Susan," she returned, "Susan Winters." While the owner stepped away to prepare her drink, she couldn't help but feel a sense of camaraderie with the other patrons, all seeking recess from their tiresome battles like herself, until he returned with a shiny glass filled with the whiskey blend she had asked for.

SKYLAND'S FINEST: WORK ONE

As Susan sipped her sour, she lingered before speaking, unsure whether to divulge her troubles to a complete stranger. Yet something about his warm, compassionate eyes made her feel at ease.

"I had a rough day at work," Susan began barely above a whisper. "I'm new at Skyland, and someone who hates me set me up to fail and embarrassed me in front of our entire team." The ache was written all over her face, and seeing this, JJ nodded as if he had heard it all before, which surprised Susan.

"People can be cruel sometimes," he added while wiping the counter with a well-worn cloth. He's seen many come with their troubles and poured many drinks to drown their sorrows, but Susan's story seemed to hold his interest.

"I just feel so let down. I mean, I don't quite know if I can trust anyone there…I'm not even sure if I should stay." Her thoughts were swirling like the melting ice in her glass, and as for JJ himself, the lines on his face deepened with uneasiness.

"It's tough, I know. But you can't let one person's actions drive you away from your passion," he said. He meant well. However, some issues need time to mend and perhaps another drink to wash them down. Then, while JJ searched for a glass to polish for tomorrow's customer, Susan glanced up to discover a familiar person broadcasting from the television box just above the bar. Her voice filled the tavern, capturing the attention of everyone present, and as the two tuned in, there she was, Vanessa Rooney, reporting on the conclusive events that had unfolded in Freeland near the day's end.

"Is that the woman behind your troubles?" he asked.

"Yup, that's her. She's the one who set me up, leading me on a ridiculous goose hunt at the public archive center." The gorgeous yet rotten anchor captivated her viewers with

SKYLAND'S FINEST: WORK ONE

sheer confidence, leaving no room for doubt about her talent. Watching the trickster at her finest, even Susan couldn't deny her skill in front of the camera, and as Vanessa went on, she couldn't help but feel a pang of bitterness, knowing that the woman on the screen would soon be claiming the lead anchor position at Skyland News.

"You know, talent can take you far, but it's character that truly matters in the end." Susan took a moment, then looked to him for answers.

"Do you really think so?" Patting the glass to a shine, he nodded in reassurance before speaking.

"Absolutely. Talent may open doors, but it's how you treat others, and the choices you make, that define who you are." Susan reflected on his words deeply, and as Vanessa's voice gradually faded into the backdrop, our young journalist realized that her story was far from over.

A COUNCILMAN'S DILEMMA

SKYLAND'S FINEST: WORK ONE

In a historical property featuring lofty ceilings, lustrous marble floors, and intricate windows along the walls draped in velvet, the Councilman's office found its advantage on the highest storey among power and influence within the city's political landscape, presenting an impressive view of Freeland's horizon and the city's streets below.

During which the last remnants of daylight faded beyond its outlooks, and as one approached his study, the designation "Bancroft" was elegantly etched on the glass panel built into the door, distinguishing his influential role within the local government.

Upon entering, a myriad of credentials, noteworthy mentions, and photographic moments of the man's public service testified to his dedication and impact on the community.

The interior was tastefully furnished with rich wood paneling, first-rate leather chairs, and antique furnishings that contributed to an atmosphere of refinement and gravitas.

A COUNCILMAN'S DILEMMA

Fine art pieces added a touch of cultured indulgence to the space even as rich mahogany bookshelves stood proudly, housing leather-bound volumes of legal texts, historical tomes, and political literature, reflecting a well-rounded individual with a passion for governance.

But at the edge of an expansive, polished oak desk, a brass nameplate proudly displayed his full name and years in office, hinting at the countless decisions and deliberations that had occurred within those walls.

But then, in this late hour, Freeland's distant sounds mingling with the muffled hush of the office was shattered by the rustling of Bancroft, himself, gathering his belongings.

He was in trouble. He quickly donned his weather coat while carefully tucking a crucial instrument in his pocket when—

RING, RING, RING!

"Not now."

RING, RING, RING!

SKYLAND'S FINEST: WORK ONE

He was so close to leaving what troubled him at his desk. Nonetheless, the Councilman carefully made his way to the shrilling noiseness. Apprehension grew with each step, and as he drew closer, he mustered the courage to pick up the receiver.

"Bancroft speaking." His voice trembled with worry creeping through his veins.

The caller's voice crackled through the corded connection, rattling Bancroft's spirit. Nervousness began to etch lines of worry across his face as his facade crumbled, revealing the internal unrest he had fought to conceal.

As the call continued, his eyes darted around the room, betraying a sense of concern as he struggled to comprehend the gravity of the situation. His hand clenched the device almost desperately despite the knuckles turning white as his grip tightened.

Each word from the mysterious caller seemed to affect him physically, as if holding

A COUNCILMAN'S DILEMMA

on to the receiver gave him a tenuous connection to the unraveling threads of his once-secure existence.

Then, as the weight of the situation began to hang heavily in the air, Bancroft's heart nearly stopped when the mysterious caller closed the call, leaving the Councilman alone at the drone of the dial tone.

PANIC TAKES HOLD

PANIC TAKES HOLD

As the night wore on, the journalist and the barkeeper's pleasant exchange continued, delving into the depths of dreams, destinations, funny real-time moments, and the power of staying true to oneself.

For Susan, it was like a tiny spark of joy to explore new ideas and comedic scenarios with someone who sought the same, and she embraced every second of it leading up to the end of the tavern's operating hours.

"Oh, my goodness, look at the time." Digging into her purse, she retrieves enough cash to cover her tab, along with an extra small sum to cover the pleasurable therapy session. "I need to get some rest for tomorrow at Skyland."

Thankful for Susan and their remarkable friendship, JJ simply raises a hand to bid her a fair night.

"And if you ever need another whiskey sour, you know where to find me."

"10-4!"

SKYLAND'S FINEST: WORK ONE

With that, Susan left the tavern, ready to carve her own path and make her mark on the world, just as Nancy Mae had done before her.

#

Bancroft's breath became a ragged strain in the quiet night as he embarked on an expedition of anticipation through the streets of Freeland. A patchwork of shadows fluttered across the public walkways along the path as the lines between hunter and hunted blurred. Panic had crept into the edges of his mind, but as the moments ticked by, he accepted that he was alone in this fight.

An artful glance over his shoulder uncovered a wraith and bits of his identity exposed under the harsh moonlight. With each step the Councilman took, the conviction he had worn throughout his career began to slip, revealing the powerless man beneath.

PANIC TAKES HOLD

Come what may, he needed to find an out, but where could he go? Yesturday's Jukebox Diner and several other stores were closed, sealed behind commercial locksets and storefront shutters, offering little refuge from the unknown threat.

But then, assuming the cunning of a fox, Bancroft quickly veered into an artery of the city's hidden veins—an alley. The limited passage accepted him like a serpentine's grip, pulling him and his foe into its depths. He became the architect of the maze and weaver of a potential trap, and it was in that constricted stretch where Bancroft confronted destiny.

"Still serving the brotherhood, Monroe?"

"I have made a solemn vow, Councilman, and you have spilled our secrets."

"Yes…I did, and you will be held to that agreement." Monroe's sights never left the Councilman. Thus stirring him to mock the wicked organization he once served. "How many more Messengers are left?"

SKYLAND'S FINEST: WORK ONE

Armed with a razor-edged letter opener, the death dealer stood before him, and with a steady hand, Bancroft retrieved his own harbinger, a twin to that of Monroe's.

"We are many, and you will not survive the night, Elliott Bancroft."

"I've been where you are standing, eager to spill blood for your masters, for I am one of the original Messengers, and I am prepared to expose the *Inked Brotherhood* even if it costs me my life."

Hence, they became gladiators in this narrow arena bound by a silent accord. Their weapons were not just tools but extensions of their wills, symbolizing the clash of ideologies, loyalties, and fortunes.

"For the Brotherhood."

FROM MYSTERY TO MURDER

SKYLAND'S FINEST: WORK ONE

As Susan left the cozy tavern, the night had fallen entirely upon Freeland, enveloping it in its vast cloak not before a soft drizzle of rain began to fall, creating a quiet and serene atmosphere around her.

Having felt down and discouraged earlier that afternoon, the encouraging words of the city's favored barkeeper profoundly affected Skyland's new journalist, reminding her that there were still good people in the world.

Launer Street, a direct route to her apartment blocks ahead, led her into the unexpected when she was forewarned by a faint, anguished groan emanating from a nearby alley, followed by the sharp sound of forceful strikes piercing through the stillness of the night.

Her breath became a delicate mist, forming in the cool air with each exhale. The distant groans grew urgent, tugging at the edges of her resolve. Yet, the warmth of JJ's helpful sendoff suddenly wrapped around her like a protective shawl, enabling her spirit to push through her fears. Susan knew the night concealed more than it revealed, and there she stood, tilting on the ridge of discovery. Yet, with a steadying breath, she stepped towards the alleyway, her voice slicing through the silence once more.

"Hello!" Her heart hammered against her chest, a staccato rhythm that matched the quickening tempo of unseen struggles. "Do you need medical attention?" she called out.

"Argh…"

The person's likely despair grew louder, begging someone of bravery to investigate. Thus, Susan, summoning her newfound courage, darted in, determined not to let herself be deterred by worry or doubt.

The rain falling around her intensified, and as tension seemed to encircle her, she ventured deeper.

But when she reached the juncture, she stumbled upon a chilling sight—

SKYLAND'S FINEST: WORK ONE

"Oh my." Instantly, Susan gasped at a man sprawled on the stony, bloodstained walkway beneath him.

"I-I'm parting."

"I'm here to help," she assured him. But, when she leaned closer, she recognized the victim as the Councilman, Elliott, to be exact. "No, no, no, no…no."

Clinging to each breath washed away by the rain, Bancroft formed his sights in the direction of the far end of the alley, whispering a name that sent a quake down Susan's backbone.

"The Messenger…"

"Messenger…what is even that?"

Struggling to process his dying words, Susan then froze at the presence of Bancroft's attacker clad in a lengthy coat to conceal his figure, black gloves for engaging, a tattered scarf to brave the cold, and a wool flat cap over his noggin to mask his identity.

SHINK!

FROM MYSTERY TO MURDER

"You made a grave mistake discovering our presence," he declared. His voice seeped with toxin. The soaring bricks around them became his to control, and now, with a witness on his trail, Monroe prepared his weapon to neutralize all risks involved. "For the Brotherhood."

Trapped between dread and urgency, Susan stretched over the Councilman to shield him from further harm until weighted footsteps, along with a reassuring hand on her shoulder, made known the unexpected arrival of the renowned Detective.

"Stay with him, Susan; I'll take it from here," came a commanding voice.

Startled, Susan looked up to find none other than—

"Michael Gibson?"

"That's right."

She was shocked by the judgment emanating from his powerful stance but reassured that Freeland's hero would catch his man.

SKYLAND'S FINEST: WORK ONE

Covering Bancroft, Susan watched as Michael dashed after the elusive Messenger down the deep depths of the rainy night, hoping the powers behind the Councilman's collapse had ultimately met their match.

And so, as the echoes of the chase died away, she found herself alone with the significance of the revelation finally unmasked—the Councilman, whom she had adored and admired, was not just a public figure but a beloved friend.

The rain continued to fall in the background as the man whom she had looked up to her entire age was now fighting for his life in her arms. He was her source of inspiration and undoubtedly the one who shaped her into the daring individual she had become.

"Grandpa."

MIDNIGHT REVELATIONS

SKYLAND'S FINEST: WORK ONE

The wooden door creaked open, allowing a foggy gust of rain-soaked air to enter. The warming enclosure was without a sound where Susan Winters, having survived her appalling encounter with the Messenger, had sought solace under the comforting ambiance of JJ's Tavern.

Her thoughts were entangled in a web of suspicion, sorrow, and uncertainty, and as she looked up from her trembling hands, her eyes met with those of two police officers who intended to collect her side of this story.

"Evening, Jerry," spoke the mildest of the two.

"Brian," he addressed explicitly. Jerry, again known as JJ among his regulars, stood tall behind the bar like a reassuring anchor amid the brewing storm outside, encouraging Susan to remain calm during the event's tragedy that had followed her indoors.

Soaked with curiosity and suspicion, the two men in uniform scanned the bar, during

MIDNIGHT REVELATIONS

which their silver badges flashed at an angle just under the warm lights overhead. Meanwhile, the wet whispers and hushed conversations among their unit outside, disputing the whereabouts of Bancroft's killer, trickled in via their radios seen at the hip.

Suddenly, Brian aimed to cut through the tense silence by summoning his first suspect.

"Miss, my partner and I believe you may have witnessed something crucial to our investigation…are you willing to cooperate at this moment?"

Susan's palms were clammy with the mark of worry, and her heart was still throbbing from the tragic episode as she looked up to JJ to intervene.

"Look, fellas, this young lady has been through enough tonight," he stated, "Give her some time to collect her thoughts before you start, got it?" Brian, gazing ever so slightly, aversely agreed.

"Perhaps another time then, Jerry," said

SKYLAND'S FINEST: WORK ONE

Brian as he and his partner returned to the tavern's creaking wooden door.

"Yeah, another time," said JJ, and as they watched on, Susan overheard them mention the Detective and, in consequence, strengthened her reason to return to Skyland.

"I heard Michael's been assigned to this case, and If anyone can unravel this messy mystery, it's him."

SUSAN'S PERSISTENCE

SKYLAND'S FINEST: WORK ONE

The air crackled with urgency as Susan marched into the newsroom, and reaching Skyland's Chief Editor was her top priority. Amidst the chaos of copy clerks, teletypists, task editors, and layout artists organizing the next morning's paper, she could sense their gazes and doubtful whispers regarding her shocking encounter the night before.

Monitoring Susan's advance, a wary copy editor with a fixed posture began to follow her with concern. Hence, as she drew near a familiar juncture, he intercepted her.

"Uh, Susan, he is in a private meeting at the moment. Maybe you should wait before barging in there."

"Not now, Larry!" Ignoring his warning, Susan pushed onward, and barging in, she did.

BAM!

Startled, Dennis and Vanessa looked up from their hushed chatter, bent with surprise and met with importance.

SUSAN'S PERSISTENCE

Her sudden intrusion tempted the news team to abandon their desks, eager to participate in the fuss unfolding. Meantime, Jane watched from the sidelines, torn between her loyalty to Skyland's workplace guidelines and her growing admiration for Susan's unwavering tenacity.

"There's more to the death of the Councilman, I swear it."

Standing before the Chief Editor of Skyland News was his new hire, appealing for a hand in the story she experienced personally. Skeptical somewhat, Dennis held his thoughts until Vanessa, leaning against the nearest wall just under a clock, met Susan with disbelief, evident in her voice smudged with spite.

"Here we go," she teased. Even so, Dennis had wrapped up his beliefs and sat up to offer his opinion on the matter.

"Look, Susan, I understand that you're upset, and I appreciate your passion for seeking justice for the Councilman, but we can't publish an exposé based solely on a hunch. We need tangible evidence to back it up. Otherwise, we risk our reputation."

"But I saw the killer!" All be it true, she was there during her grandfather's dying moments, but divulging this information would be her undoing in stealing this story.

"Dennis is right," Vanessa added. "We can't afford another wild goose."

"Yeah, a wild goose chase you sent me on, Vanessa!"

"Are you sure you're not just trying to get back at me?"

"Alright that's enough, girls! Let's approach this prospect with some reason." Frustrated beyond the surface, Susan sought to maintain her composure before rejoining the discussion.

"Vanessa, this isn't about you. It's about exposing the truth and bringing justice to those involved. Besides, even the great Detective Michael Gibson was there!"

SUSAN'S PERSISTENCE

"Wait, wait, wait! You actually met Michael?" The mere mention of the great Detective sparked something within him, and his skepticism momentarily disappeared, replaced by a childlike enthusiasm.

"Yes!"

"The legendary investigator, you mean? The man who's solved hundreds of baffling cases?"

"That's what I'm trying to declare here, and I can confidently affirm that he was everything Jane had described him to be!"

Unimpressed by Dennis's sudden passion for Freeland's hero, Vanessa rolled her eyes, shifting her attention away from their interaction. Furthermore, he couldn't contain his voice as it rose with each word.

"Girls, do you know what this means?"

"And what does this mean, Dennis?"

Rattling at the opportunity brewing within the room, Vanessa was reminded of her ongoing motives in becoming Skyland's—

SKYLAND'S FINEST: WORK ONE

"It means that Susan may have a direct line to the greatest Detective of our time!"

"And *our* next breaking story!"

"Exactly!" Taken aback by Dennis's elated response, Susan couldn't help but encourage his eagerness. It was as if a switch had been flipped, turning him into an overenthusiastic fanboy.

"Susan, jot down every detail about your encounter with Michael Gibson. What he was wearing, what was said—did he have a gun?"

Thoroughly annoyed at this point, the stormy anchor interrupted their conversation with an exasperated sigh, following a spiteful nudge in hopes of derailing Susan's chance at this lead.

"Oh please, Dennis. Let's not get carried away here. We need indisputable facts that she actually saw this creepy thin-man freak instead of relying on the musings of a master Detective."

Undeterred by Vanessa's false assertions,

SUSAN'S PERSISTENCE

Dennis continued to revel in his newfound joy, mimicking the hero's stride around his office, occasionally pretending to inspect his smokey command for hidden danger.

"Lookout, my dear Vanessa! We're onto something big here," he claimed. "Susan!" he aimed, "You must follow this lead, even if it means diving in headfirst, got it?"

"You got it, Dennis."

When their partnership began high above Freeland in Skyland's glorious Sky-Bird, Susan's fate took on a dramatic twist, and despite the challenges she had faced thus far, she couldn't let one person stop her from uncovering the secrets beyond her grandfather's execution, and perhaps, becoming Skyland's Finest along the way.

To Be Continued...

BECOMING WANTED

SKYLAND'S FINEST: WORK ONE

Becoming Susan was a truly transformative journey that felt instinctive yet grew over time. Initially, portraying her felt a bit awkward since she was my first character. But with the support and encouragement of a dear friend, I wholeheartedly embraced the role and realized that I personified her perfectly.

David Geary's openness to incorporate my talent and insights into the character added immense value to his directing style, and as a result, stepping into the shoes of Skyland's courageous journalist felt the part was always meant for me.

In conclusion, I am deeply grateful for the opportunity and the collaborative spirit that brought Susan to life, marking both a personal and professional milestone and leaving an indelible mark on my heart.

Rock *Ill*

THE COUNCILMAN'S CURSE

THE COUNCILMAN'S CURSE

As the train rumbled along the tracks, the city of Freeland blurred past her through the window of her car compartment, doing little to ease the unrest brewing within her. Susan couldn't shake the gnawing feeling that she had stumbled upon something truly sinister, and with Dennis supporting her, she found herself inextricably connected to the dark undercurrents that had changed the course of her life and her career as a journalist.

Arriving at Samson Railway Station, the first traces of twilight dangled over the vacant post. The day's operations had wound down, and the station staff had clocked out. Travelers had trickled away, leaving only the echo of Susan's heels clicking against the cold platform, for she was the last to disembark the train heading East.

The last of daylight clung to the world as Susan returned home, and while the spirit of nightfall wormed through the windows of her apartment, our brave journalist retreated to the shower to confront her grief once more. She didn't foresee any of this. In the beginning, she was offered a fantastic opportunity to work for Freeland's proudest news station. But then, just as danger quickly discovered her, Elliott's demise had already made it to the front page of Skyland's Insider.

Leading into the living room unthinkingly, Susan eventually noticed an unexpected sight amidst the simple, period-appropriate setting—her tape recorder, bathing in the moon's streaming beams. The device hadn't been there when she left, and she couldn't recall removing it from the nightstand earlier that week.

A rare chill trickled down her shoulders as she hesitated. But curiosity got the better of her, as revealed by a wet trail on the floorboards beneath her bare feet. This observation could change the course of her investigation and possibly her life, but she couldn't fight the urge to turn away.

THE COUNCILMAN'S CURSE

With trembling fingers, she pressed play, and as the tape recorder whirred to life, a familiar voice sealed the room, causing her blood to run cold.

"Well, Susan, aren't we having a joyous time chasing stories."

"Oh my God," she gasped. The voice's menacing drawl seized her fearlessness, entangling her with its nefarious tendrils since the moment the playback began.

"I've anticipated you to become a delicate thorn in my side. But I must admit, you have shown a tenacity that is... quite remarkable."

"You were in my — when? How?" she asked the empty room.

The articulated agent, dripping with terrifying egotism, paused, allowing the silence to amplify the growing terror in her chest.

"The Councilman uttered our existence, an awful mistake he has taken to his grave."

"How dare you?"

SKYLAND'S FINEST: WORK ONE

Tears began to flow from Susan's eyes as she remembered her grandfather's final moments. Yet, despite this, an impulsive spark of determination began to radiate from within her while the grim transmission continued to circulate.

"Consider this a warning: do not pursue us, or the citizens of Freeland will learn of your end in the next day's paper."

www.becomewanted.com

www.ingramcontent.com/pod-product-compliance
Lightning Source LLC
LaVergne TN
LVHW021952060526
838201LV00049B/1676